Dear Parent:

Congratulations! Your child is taking the first steps on an exciting journey. The destination? Independent reading!

STEP INTO READING® will help your child get there. The program offers books at five levels that accompany children from their first attempts at reading to reading success. Each step includes fun stories, fiction and nonfiction, and colorful art. There are also Step into Reading Sticker Books, Step into Reading Math Readers, and Step into Reading Phonics Readers— a complete literacy program with something to interest every child.

Learning to Read, Step by Step!

Ready to Read   Preschool–Kindergarten
• big type and easy words • rhyme and rhythm • picture clues
For children who know the alphabet and are eager to begin reading.

Reading with Help   Preschool–Grade 1
• basic vocabulary • short sentences • simple stories
For children who recognize familiar words and sound out new words with help.

Reading on Your Own   Grades 1–3
• engaging characters • easy-to-follow plots • popular topics
For children who are ready to read on their own.

Reading Paragraphs   Grades 2–3
• challenging vocabulary • short paragraphs • exciting stories
For newly independent readers who read simple sentences with confidence.

Ready for Chapters   Grades 2–4
• chapters • longer paragraphs • full-color art
For children who want to take the plunge into chapter books but still like colorful pictures.

STEP INTO READING® is designed to give every child a successful reading experience. The grade levels are only guides. Children can progress through the steps at their own speed, developing confidence in their reading, no matter what their grade.

Remember, a lifetime love of reading starts with a single step!

www.seussville.com www.catinthehat.com www.stepintoreading.com

Educators and librarians, for a variety of teaching tools, visit us at www.randomhouse.com/teachers

Library of Congress Cataloging-in-Publication Data
Worth, Bonnie.
Cooking with the cat / by Bonnie Worth ; illustrated by Christopher Moroney. — 1st Random House ed.
    p.   cm. — (Step into reading. A step 1 book)
"Based on the motion picture screenplay by Alec Berg & David Mandel & Jeff Schaffer."
SUMMARY: The Cat in the Hat bakes cupcakes in this simple retelling of a scene from the movie version of Dr. Seuss's classic book.
ISBN 0-375-82494-4 (trade) — ISBN 0-375-92494-9 (lib. bdg.)
[1. Cookery—Fiction. 2. Cats—Fiction. 3. Stories in rhyme.]
I. Moroney, Christopher, ill. II. Title. III. Series: Step into reading. Step 1 book.
PZ8.3.W896 Co 2003 [E]—dc21 2003007281

Printed in the United States of America First Edition 10 9 8 7 6 5 4 3 2 1

STEP INTO READING®

STEP 1

Cooking with the Cat

By Bonnie Worth
Illustrated by Christopher Moroney

Based on the motion picture screenplay by
Alec Berg & David Mandel & Jeff Schaffer

Based on the book by Dr. Seuss

Random House 🏠 New York

Look! Look!
The Cat wants
to cook!

Look! A book!

The Cat has

a cookbook!

COOKING WITH THE CAT

By the Cat in the Hat

We need
a tin!

Which tin
will win?

The thin tin
is best.
Put back
the rest.

We need
ham and jam.

12

Lots and lots
of pots.

We spot
the pot!

15

Hot shot
into the pot.

A pot shot!

(Not so hot!)

We take
a seat.
We start
to beat.

No, no, no!
We do not eat
the treat
we beat.

Do not

slop

the glop

on top.

Stop! Stop!

Stop that glop!

Mop up
that glop!

Do not

drop

the mop

in glop!

We heat
the treat.

A spot
on the pot!

Got the pot!

Ding!

They are done.

A neat seat
to eat a treat!

We eat
and eat
and eat
and eat!